GLORIA HUTCHINSON

The HEART'S HEALING JOURNEY

Seeking Desert Wisdom

St. Anthony Messenger Press

Cincinnati, Ohio

Abbey of Gethsemani. Reprinted by permission of New Directions Publishing Corp.

Excerpt from *Selected Poetry of Jessica Powers*, edited by Regina Siegfried, A.S.C., and Robert F. Morneau, copyright ©1989 by Sheed & Ward, reprinted by permission of Sheed & Ward.

Reprinted from *Holiness* by Donald Nicholl, copyright ©1981 and 1987 by Paulist Press. Used by permission of Paulist Press.

Excerpt from *The Enlightened Heart: An Anthology of Sacred Poetry*, edited by Stephen Mitchell, copyright ©1989 by Stephen Mitchell, used by permission of HarperCollins Publishers.

Excerpts from *Meister Eckhart: A Modern Translation* by Raymond Bernard Blakney, copyright ©1941 by Harper & Brothers, copyright renewed, used by permission of HarperCollins Publishers.

Excerpts from *Conjectures of a Guilty Bystander* by Thomas Merton, copyright ©1968 by Image Books, used by permission of Doubleday.

Excerpt from *Poems of Gerard Manley Hopkins*, third edition, edited by W.H. Gardner, copyright ©1948 by Oxford University Press, Inc., used by permission of Oxford University Press, Inc.

Cover and inside illustrations by Mary Newell DePalma
Cover and book design by Mary Alfieri

ISBN 0-86716-259-7

Copyright ©1995, Gloria Hutchinson

Published by St. Anthony Messenger Press
Printed in the U.S.A.

▼

▼

▼

You desire truth in the inward being;

therefore teach me wisdom in my

secret heart.

—Psalm 51:6

▼

▼

▼

▼

For my granddaughter,

Kirsten Ann,

that Wisdom

may make a

home in her

Contents

Introduction

WE ALL SEEK WISDOM whether we know her by name or not. Some call her Meaning; others call her Enlightenment. She is the one who sees the way and guides others in it. Pilgrims whose hearts are weary or afflicted seek out Wisdom's house.

In the Russian Orthodox tradition, Wisdom is embodied by the starets, a spiritual father or mother. She is ordained for the ministry of direction by the Holy Spirit. It is not the institutional Church that invites the starets to serve. Rather, her gift is recognized and enlisted by those around her.

Like the Desert Fathers and Mothers of fifth-century Egypt and Scete, the starets is one who has wrenched himself free from society's grasp and has gone apart to find God in silence, prayer and self-emptying. Having attained inner peace, he lights a candle in his window for those trying to find their way home.

The teacher of wisdom is a man or woman of few words. When a seeker comes asking for a "word" by which to live, the spiritual elder may respond with a parable, an enigmatic saying or a question. The response is not a prepared text but a Spirit-shaped utterance. Out of the ensuing dialogue comes discernment.

For example, consider the young person who approaches a Desert Mother saying, "A certain one has spread rumors about me and sullied my good name. Am I not justified in gaining my revenge?" The elder responds, "You could send her roses or bake her a cake." The young person, listening from the heart, will grasp the "word": *Because the gossiper has offered you an opportunity to grow in humility, to stop imagining that you are a sterling character beyond reproach, you should reward this person. She has served as your spiritual director.*

Whether the wisdom teacher is Hasidic or Sufi, Greek Orthodox or Native American, Zen Buddhist or Roman Catholic, he or she consults the same ultimate Source. The house of Wisdom is accessible to every human heart.

When an elder was asked about a certain course of action, he said, "Do not take one course or the other until you ask your heart if what you propose to do is according to God." Here we take the elder's advice. Our communal "yes" gives birth to Amma Sophia, the feminine figure of Wisdom personified in these pages as a Christian hermit. She is a physician of the soul whose words of life can effect the heart's healing.

To Sophia comes Lucien, a contemporary married Christian whose comfortable life leaves him vaguely sick at heart. Having gained the world, he desires more. He looks to the Amma to heal whatever ails him.

It is perhaps no coincidence that Lucien's name is rooted in the ancient Anglo-Saxon "locian" (to look) and the Latin "lumen" (light).

1
APPROACHING WISDOM'S DWELLING

Lucien seeks out Sophia as physician for his soul.

H E HAS COME A LONG WAY, with himself the greatest obstacle to attaining his destination. "Wait until this holy woman finds out that you are simply an average person who can't be satisfied with what he's already got," the inner skeptic warns him. "You, with your wonderful family, your business success, your pillar-of-the-parish reputation. What more do you want out of life?"

Ignoring the voice, Lucien jogs toward the clearing where the hermitage becomes visible. A canopy of lordly pines covers him, and he smiles at the memory of himself as a third grader at St. Bruno's School singing "His Banner Over Me Is Love."

Now, more than ever, the seeker is assured that he was right to take his pastor's advice. Father Andrew had sensed that Lucien needed more than an annual retreat or a good book on spiritual direction. "Go to Amma Sophia," he advised. "She sees into the heart." In that moment, embraced by the quiet, Lucien is thankful that the priest was not one to dismiss a little spiritual heart trouble the way some people ignore a "harmless" skin cancer or a chronic cough.

He approaches the hermitage as though he were stalking a deer. "What if the Amma is lost in contemplation?" Reports of her holiness grip him like restraining hands. "Why is it that holiness has the same effect on us as a royal banquet set with an intimidating array of cutlery? Both attract us from afar and rattle us on contact. I simply want to sit at the Amma's table. But the sweat running down my sides says, 'Back off. You're out of your element here.'"

The simplicity of the log hermitage is reassuring, however. His knock is answered immediately by a voice from the garden.

"Hello! I'm out here."

Lucien's first sight of Amma Sophia is instructive. In her faded work dress, straw hat and sandals, she could be a Salvadoran peasant. Her dark hair is pulled up out of harm's way. Her hand, extended in welcome, is as rough as a carpenter's. Holiness now seems more like a spontaneous picnic than a royal banquet. Sophia's voice, deep and musical, makes him glad he did not turn back.

When they are settled at the table with mugs of coffee, homemade bread and raspberry jam, the Amma invites Lucien to join her in silent prayer. Then she begins without benefit of small talk.

"Time is a sacramental. Honor its sacred character, and it will draw you into the arms of God. Fritter it away, and you are a child crying over your skinned knee while refusing your mother's embrace. Why have you come?"

"My life is full, but my heart feels hollow," Lucien answers. "I think I'm a good person, yet I might just be going through the motions. Am I a believer—or a hypocrite? I went to our family doctor—in case there might be a physical cause of my anxieties. But he says there's nothing wrong with me. What do you think?"

Sophia is silent. The brassy *dee-dee-dee* of a chickadee in the window feeder invites Lucien not to take himself too seriously.

"If you had an abscessed tooth, would you consult a cardiologist? The true healing you seek comes only from the divine Physician."

"And I am here because I believe that the divine Physician may heal me through you. I have intelligence, goodwill and common sense. What I lack is wisdom—the wisdom to know God and to know how to live so that when death comes I will not suddenly discover that I have only existed or acted out a part."

"A poet once reflected on how we try to free ourselves from this very sense of strangeness and alienation which you fear. He asked, 'This life—who lives it really? God, do you?' "[1] "I'd answer 'no,' " Lucien is quick to respond. "My life is too crammed with things that have nothing to do with God and everything to do with keeping myself and my family secure. Can you give me a word that will help me?"

Amma Sophia rises from her bench, signs the cross on Lucien's forehead, and says, "Each morning before arising, ask yourself: 'Am I a citizen of Jerusalem or Babylon?' Live that day according to your answer."

> *I learned both what is secret and what is*
> *manifest,*
> *for wisdom, the fashioner of all things,*
> *taught me.*

Wisdom 7:21-22

---

[1] Rainer Maria Rilke, "Although, as from a prison walled with hate," *Poems From the Book of Hours*, trans. Babette Deutsch (New York: New Directions Pub. Corp., 1941), p. 39.

2
AT WISDOM'S DOOR

*Sophia confirms that
life is meaningful.*

"HAVE YOU DECIDED to which city you belong?" Amma Sophia inquires. Lucien is pleased with her directness. He respects a physician who holds the patient accountable for carrying out the prescribed therapy.

"I am a citizen of Jerusalem," he responds. "There's no denying that I've spent too many years paying allegiance to Babylon—prizing success, bowing to material idols, going along with a culture that often contradicts the gospel. But this past week I've tried to act on my desire to do right." He then feels compelled to add, "Unfortunately, I've failed more than once."

"Ah, Lucien, are you greater than the apostle Paul who complained that he did not the good he wanted to do but the evil he did not intend? The heart is swaddled in a hundred layers. It cannot be unwrapped in a single afternoon."

Lucien nods, but his expression betrays a disciple's frustration. Into the chasm between the ideal and the real, many have fallen.

"A young woman once consulted me because she wanted to become a hermit," Amma offers. "She was all excited about the prospect of building a hermitage in the woods near here.

'How long will it take me to reach the necessary stage of spiritual maturity?' she inquired. 'Ten or twelve years,' I told her. 'You must be kidding! That long?' Then I admitted that perhaps I was wrong. 'It might be safer to say twenty.' Needless to say, the young woman was not pleased. 'But you just made it even worse.' I smiled. 'I should have said twenty-five.' "

Lucien grins as Sophia notes that the young woman made a hasty departure and has not been seen since. After a time of quiet, the Amma speaks.

"What is the aim of your life? What is its meaning?"

"I want to be an authentic Christian and to get centered on God rather than on my own selfish concerns."

"So you wish to become your original self?"

When the seeker agrees, Sophia recalls a story told by Thomas Merton about a tiger cub who was reared by wild goats. One day the cub got lost in the jungle where he encountered a full-grown tiger. Seeing the cub acting like a goat, the tiger knocked him halfway across the jungle. Examining his own life, Merton observed, "I meet a tiger in myself who is not familiar, who says, 'Choose!' and knocks me halfway across the jungle."[1]

"If you wear out Wisdom's doorstep, Lucien, you will know how to choose," the Amma assures him.

The seeker wonders if that means he will then be counted among the spiritually mature.

Sophia responds, "That depends."

"On what?"

"On whether you gaze only at the heavens or at yourself as well."

Lucien's look of impatience requires the Amma to be more explicit. "Our knowledge of God comes first from reflecting on what God does in us. By attending to the pattern of our daily encounters with the Divine, we become more intimate with the Holy One."

"How will I know that it is God acting in my life?" Lucien inquires. "Might it not be chance or good timing?"

The Amma advises him that he should listen to Julian of Norwich, who held that "Nothing happens by chance, but by the far-sighted wisdom of God." Those who refuse to see how God "lovingly brings all that happens to its best end" are "blind and blinkered."[2]

"That seems somewhat naive to me," Lucien ventures.

"The way to wisdom is the slow lane," Sophia responds, implying that the seeker has yet to find the pace.

She then presses into Lucien's hand a length of heavy twine and some wooden beads. "To dispense practical wisdom to their disciples, the ancient rabbis strung together a series of brief mental pictures or parables. We can see Jesus creating *charaz*—a string of beads—when he paints the fallen sparrows and lost strands of hair to assure us of our worth in God's eyes." (See Matthew 10:28-33.)

Sophia instructs Lucien to add a bead to the twine each time he catches God acting in his life to teach him the ways of wisdom.

> *Wisdom has built her house…*
> *she has also set her table.*
>
> Proverbs 9:1, 2

---

[1] Thomas Merton, *Conjectures of a Guilty Bystander* (Garden City, N.Y.: Image Books, 1968), p. 198.

[2] Julian of Norwich, *Daily Readings With Julian of Norwich, Vol. I* (Springfield, Ill.: Templegate Publishers, 1980), p. 26.

3
THE SPIRIT'S WORK

*Lucien invokes the Spirit's
transforming power.*

A S SOON AS AMMA SOPHIA SITS down at the table, Lucien unburdens himself by recounting an incident in which he realized, too late, that God had attempted to speak to him through a "chance" encounter with a former employee. The seeker spares himself no blame as he describes how he missed the unspoken plea for help in the man's casual account of his present circumstances. "What do you think, Amma?" Lucien inquires eagerly. "Is this a bead worth stringing?"

Without a word, Sophia rises and goes out into the garden. Lucien follows, feeling much less sure of himself. He sees her bend over and tug laboriously at a fifty-pound bag of seeds. "What are you doing?" he asks.

"I am going to carry this bag to the far end of the garden."

"But you can't do that alone."

Sophia straightens up and points an emphatic finger at Lucien. "Neither can you make spiritual progress. Today you ignored our customary space of silence before beginning our inner work. You are like a man who sets out to climb a mountain when he is already out of breath."

Lucien bows slightly. "You are right, Amma. I acted out of my usual habits of independence as a self-made man. But there aren't any self-made saints, are there?"

Smiling her appreciation, Sophia returns to the hermitage where the two enter into silent reflection. She then observes, "Remember, Lucien, no one can be a friend of the Spirit who is not a patient listener."

"Silence is difficult for me. I'm an action person who likes to get things done."

Sophia quotes an ancient Camaldolese hermit who said, "The house of God grows in sacred silence, and a temple that will never fall is constructed without noises."[1] She then adds, "That's the kind of action God calls you to now."

The Amma counsels Lucien to set his alarm clock twenty minutes earlier than usual six days a week. In that time, he is to do nothing but wait upon the Spirit. No matter how pointless the exercise seems, he is to be faithful to it. "Like the poet," she says, you are to "keep the vigil of mystery,/earthless and still."[2]

Sophia then tells Lucien the story of a middle-aged woman who, although she much preferred the privacy and quiet of the country, was forced to move to a city apartment. When she heard the occasional nighttime merriment of her younger neighbors, she was filled with resentment and could not pray.

Months went by, and now and then the woman would see her neighbors during the day. She could not help noticing that some were hardworking but poor, others were in some way handicapped yet cheerful. Gradually, the intentions of her neighbors entered into her prayers.

After many years, an old friend came to spend the weekend with the woman. When the neighbors' music and laughter interrupted the two friends' spiritual discussion, the visitor remarked, "This must drive you crazy. How do you stand it?" The woman responded, "I have learned to hear their revelry as a reminder of our shared humanity. I pray for them and for myself—that I may be deaf to the Conniver who says, 'These others are insufferable. I must get away from them.' "

Lucien reflects on the story, then responds, "This is a parable of how the Spirit whittles away our brittle edges."

"And of the Spirit as the Agent enabling us to 'ripen from within.' "[3]

The seeker is taken with the image. He

envisions himself ripening into a disciple worthy of trust. As he closes his eyes to sustain the image, Sophia stands behind him and lays both hands firmly on his head.

"Spirit of God," Lucien prays aloud. "Anoint me with the power of resurrection. Confirm me as a disciple in formation. Heal me by your unmeasured grace."

Sophia's hands are fiery as she fortifies his prayer with deep silence.

> *Therefore I prayed, and understanding*
> *was given me;*
> *I called on God, and the spirit of*
> *wisdom came to me.*
>
> Wisdom 7:7

[1] Blessed Rudolf of Camaldoli, *Camaldolese Constitution*, 44. Cited by Thomas Merton in *The Silent Life* (New York: Farrar, Straus & Cudahy, 1957), p. 160.

[2] Jessica Powers, "To Live with the Spirit," *Selected Poetry of Jessica Powers*, eds. Regina Siegfried, A.S.C, and Robert F. Morneau (Kansas City, Mo.: Sheed & Ward, 1989), p. 38.

[3] Rainer Maria Rilke, "Called me to the one among your moments," *The Enlightened Heart: An Anthology of Sacred Poetry*, ed. Stephen Mitchell (New York: Harper & Row, 1989), p. 135.

$\underline{4}$
FEAR OF THE LORD

*Sophia recommends
fear of the Lord.*

F OR SEVERAL WEEKS Lucien does not come to the hermitage, although he has assured Sophia of his intention to return "as soon as his heavy schedule permits." Intuiting the cause of his absence, the Amma sends him the following story.

> There was a certain minnow who trembled every time a school of striped bass appeared. So he prayed to the Lord of the Fishes, and the Lord turned him into a striped bass. But then he began to have an anxiety attack whenever the marlin ventured in his direction. So the Lord turned him into a marlin. All was well until the marlin spotted a killer shark in the distance and began to cry, "Help me, Lord, or I am surely lost!" But at that point, the Lord of the Fishes gave up and said, "Enough! No matter how much I change you, you still cling to your minnow's heart." And instantly the marlin became a minnow again and trembled as he swam away.[1]

At first, Lucien dismisses the fable as having nothing to do with his spiritual search. In time, however, he begins to see how he has allowed his fears about what others may say—his family, his buddies, his colleagues—to turn him aside.

He dreads being categorized as a "religious freak" or a "holier-than-thou." Too, there is the wider fear of how his life might change if he gets close to the God who is a consuming fire.

After regaining his resolve, Lucien returns to the hermitage where Sophia welcomes him as though there had been no interruption.

"What do you fear, my friend?" she inquires.

Instinct tells him to dissimulate. But he thinks better of it and admits his apprehensions about death, physical suffering (his own or his family's), loneliness, failure.

"Do you fear that others may see you for who you really are and find you inadequate?"

"Yes, I guess I do."

"So in a sense, you fear yourself. And God too?"

"Ah, but the Bible recommends fear of the Lord!"

"Do you cling to your minnow's heart in this regard?"

Lucien laughs good-naturedly. He has never been sure how to interpret "fear of the Lord." It is a question he has avoided, not wanting to consider what kind of God needs to be feared.

"Reflect," Sophia advises, "which of the following truly fears the Lord? Is it the lawyer who obeys every law of the Church, worships every Sunday out of a sense of duty and avoids sin because he dreads winding up in hell where he presumes so many of his clients will be? Or is it the teacher who sometimes breaks Church laws, worships out of a sincere desire to do so and identifies with others as poor sinners like himself who need God's love to survive?"

Lucien immediately understands that the person who holds God in loving awe and shows God reverence of his own free will is the one who authentically fears the Lord. At last he can hear "The fear of the Lord is the beginning of wisdom" as an invitation rather than a correction.[2]

"Growth in reverence," Sophia observes, "will bring a blossoming of trust. We can gauge how significant this must be simply by counting all the times in the Gospels when Jesus insists, 'Fear not!' and 'Be not afraid' and 'Why did you fear?' Imagine how our hearts would expand if we could unmask fear and say, 'Be gone, outlaw! Jesus Christ reigns here!' "

The Amma continues to explain that Jesus in the desert brought fear into subjection by carving out a sanctuary of prayer and the word. Inviting Lucien to do likewise whenever the need arises, she sets an example with spontaneous beatitudes.

> "Blest are they who fear not what others may say; they shall be free to do what is right.

> "Blest are they who fear not what others may do; they shall be trusting and nonviolent.

> "Blest are they who fear not failure; they shall be trees that blossom in winter.

> "Blest are they who fear not what may happen tomorrow; they shall reap the harvest of today.

> "Blest are they who fear not to be alone; they shall be with God.

> "Blest are they who fear not death; they shall drink deeply at the fountain of life."

*The fear of the Lord is the crown of
wisdom,
making peace and perfect health to
flourish.*

Sirach 1:18

---

[1] See Anthony de Mello, S.J., *The Heart of the Enlightened* (New York: Doubleday, 1989), p. 16.

[2] See Psalm 111:10.

5

WALKING ON WATER

Lucien grasps the link between trust and mercy.

F AILING TO FIND AMMA SOPHIA in the hermitage or the garden, Lucien calls loudly until he hears a response from an unexpected direction. He can see patches of Sophia's blue dress through the foliage of a large oak which she has climbed to a distance of about fifteen feet. "Amma, be careful!" he shouts. "You are going to fall!"

"No, Lucien, I am going to rise."

With that, Sophia climbs onto a long branch for a purpose which remains mysterious and provoking to the observer. Then, while Lucien mutters a Hail Mary to himself, his mentor makes her descent. "May I ask why you did that?" he inquires in a parental tone.

"Because I saw a good reason to do it and no good reason not to," she replies. With that, Sophia draws forth from her apron pocket a pin-feathered baby hawk with startled eyes and open beak. Its mother had not returned for three days, and the Amma felt called to save it.

"But you should not take such chances— especially when you are here alone."

"Was Peter alone when he walked on the water?" Sophia queries.

Lucien suppresses an exasperated response

intended only to preserve the high ground for himself. Instead, he replies, "No, only when he fell."

"That's right, my friend," encourages the Amma. "Now come. We shall pray and talk while I feed this fledgling."

Lucien suspects that Sophia may have timed her rescue mission to remind him of the ways in which we are constrained by fear. His insight seems confirmed when she tells him the story of two monks who on their journey come to a river where a lovely young woman is waiting to cross. She cannot swim and is reluctant to venture forth alone.

"The first monk gets all tangled up in his thoughts about how monks must have nothing to do with women and what a scandal it will cause if he gets caught helping a woman in distress. While he is deliberating, the second monk picks up the woman and carries her to the other side. Once secure, the woman goes on her way, while the two monks proceed in silence. They have walked nearly five miles before the first monk asks, 'Why did you have anything to do with that woman back there?' And the second responds, 'Are you still carrying her? I put her down when I got across the river.' "[1]

Laughing heartily, Lucien appreciates the implied connection between mercy and trust. His heart takes pleasure in the memory of Gerard Manley Hopkins' reassuring lines: "I say that we are wound/With mercy round and round."[2]

Sophia reinforces his perception by observing that the wise "trust God wherever they go, close to shore or out deep, for no matter where they go, God is the sea that upholds them and they are drenched in mercy."

"Nor should we allow mistrust of ourselves to prevent us from showing mercy to others," adds Lucien.

Drawing on the wisdom of Gregory of Nyssa, Sophia defines mercy as the virtue that smooths out the inequalities between master and servant, rich and poor, sick and healthy, male and female.[3] Had Peter continued to trust in Christ's mercy, he, like the Rabbi himself, would have strolled across the waves.

"If only we could always trust God to keep us afloat," Lucien responds. "But experience teaches that even if we trust, we can still fall out of a tree or drown in a lake. It's just not that simple, I'm afraid."

"And what did the Lord reveal to Julian of

Norwich about that very point?"

The seeker shakes his head, regretting that he had not followed Sophia's counsel about reading *The Revelations of Divine Love*.

"He did not say, 'You shall not be tempest-tossed, you shall not be work-weary, you shall not be discomforted.' But he said, 'You shall not be overcome.' Not only does Christ love us. He likes us and has called us friends. In return, he wants us to love him, like him, and firmly trust in him."[4]

Recalling Christ's best-known promise to Julian, Lucien redeems himself by adding, "And all shall be well, and all will be well, and all manner of thing shall be well."

Sophia commends Lucien. She then places the pin-feathered hawk, now contented by earthworms and milk, in a towel-lined box. "I will care for him until he learns to fly," she says.

The seeker, departing to reflect on a psalm of mercy and trust, takes her words to heart.

> *Many are the torments of the wicked,*
> *   but steadfast love surrounds those*
> *who trust in the LORD.*
>
> Psalm 32:10

[1] See *The Wisdom of the Zen Masters*, trans. Irmgard Shloegl (New York: New Directions Pub. Corp., 1976), p. 39.

[2] Gerard Manley Hopkins, "The Blessed Virgin compared to the Air we Breathe," *Poems of Gerard Manley Hopkins*, ed. W. H. Gardner (London: Oxford University Press, 1948), p. 100.

[3] Paul Quenon, "Freedom in Progress According to St. Gregory of Nyssa," *Cistercian Studies*, Vol. XVII, No. 1, 1982, p. 17.

[4] Julian of Norwich, *Daily Readings*, pp. 53, 54.

6
BEYOND 'WHO'S RIGHT?'

*Sophia recommends that
Lucien learn to accept
being wrong.*

S ENSING A WEIGHT ON Lucien's heart, Amma
Sophia touches his shoulder lightly as she
pours the coffee. "Now you will lay this burden
down," she comments. "The pilgrim is called to
travel light."

Lucien, relieved by Sophia's intuitiveness,
explains that Father Andrew died of a heart
attack at the age of sixty. Lucien and his family
had long admired the priest. "His reputation for
holiness was known throughout the diocese. He
was my image of what a priest should be."

That image, however, became clouded when
Lucien learned from an attorney friend that
Father Andrew's estate included a luxurious
retirement residence in the mountains and a
collection of costly antiques. This apparent
appetite for worldly treasures diminished the
priest in Lucien's eyes.

"I don't know why his acquisitiveness
should make me lose heart," he rationalizes.
"After all, no one is perfect—not even those who
appear to be so holy."

Sophia's eyes are instantly ignited. "And if
we were all perfect," she asks, "would we not
rob God of the opportunity to be merciful? The
person who presumes to assess another's

holiness is like a passenger without a license who pushes God into the back seat and says, 'Here, let me do the driving.' "

Stung, Lucien is indignant. "Are you saying that we shouldn't strive to be perfect or expect others—especially the religious professionals—to do so? Whatever happened to 'Be perfect as your heavenly Father is perfect'?"[1]

Sophia allows several moments of silence to calm the atmosphere. She then speaks quietly of how "perfect" is to be interpreted in Lucien's citation. Jesus, she points out, challenges his disciples not to be perfectly sinless or perfectly law-abiding but to make continual progress toward spiritual maturity. By reflecting on our daily encounters with God, we move closer to this desired state. The Amma emphasizes that Luke's parallel verse to Matthew's requires us to "Be merciful, just as your Father is merciful."[2]

Lucien hates to let go of a belief that has served him well as armor and armament. But he has an inkling that it takes more courage to live with imperfection—our own and others'—than to focus on a superiority in which ego thrives. He says nothing, however.

"Tell me, my friend," Sophia asks, "do you need to be right?"

"I don't know if I'd call it a need. Like anyone else, I'd rather be right than wrong."

"A certain Desert Father advised a monk never to argue with anyone. He observed that if someone speaks rightly to you, say 'Yes.' If he speaks wrongly, say 'You know what you are saying.' But do not argue about what he has said. Then you will have peace of mind."[3]

Lucien is about to make a comeback but thinks better of it. Sophia approves him with a nod and continues. "Every time you feel compelled to show that you are right and another is either wrong or sinful, ask yourself 'Who am I to judge?' Give up judging and gain tranquillity of heart."

The seeker balks at this hard counsel. He insists that there are times when it is important to prove oneself right and one's opponent wrong.

Understanding his reluctance, the Amma requires him to move to higher ground. "You have not yet learned how to be wrong or to allow others to err. Do not regard errors or ignorant blunders as the vulture eyes carrion. See them through the lens of compassion, remembering that we are all earthen vessels."

Sophia invites Lucien to replace critical

judging with intelligent reading of hearts. "Reach for the proverb which teaches, 'The purposes in the human mind are like deep water / but the intelligent will draw them out.' "[4]

Entering into the spirit of the dialogue at last, Lucien draws forth from his own storehouse a teaching of the ancient Chinese philosopher Chuang Tzu: "The wise person 'sees that on both sides of every argument there is both right and wrong.' "[5]

Sophia claps her hands in appreciation. "So when will you be ready to retire from the bench, your honor?"

"Soon, I hope. Until now, I had no doubts about my ability to tell the weeds from the wheat."

"When you must judge, Lucien, do it not according to your own lights but, as Hildegard says, 'according to the motherly heart of God's mercy.' Now go in peace and be compassionate."[6]

> *All deeds are right in the sight of the*
> *doer,*
> *but the LORD weighs the heart.*
>
> Proverbs 21:2

[1] See Matthew 5:48.

[2] Luke 6:36.

[3] See Thomas Merton, *The Wisdom of the Desert* (New York: New Directions Pub. Corp., 1960), p. 29.

[4] Proverbs 20:5.

[5] Thomas Merton, *The Way of Chuang Tzu* (New York: New Directions Pub. Corp., 1965), p. 43.

[6] Barbara Newman, *Sister of Wisdom: St. Hildegard's Theology of the Feminine* (Berkeley, Calif.: University of California Press, 1987), p. 231.

7

MEDICINE FOR THE HEART

*Lucien repents and embraces
his Mother Jesus.*

FINGERING A NEW BEAD he had strung on his twine, Lucien relates how he welcomed a young friend of his daughter's into his home with cold charity. "I spoke politely to her and told her to make herself at home. All the while I was telling myself that she was too assertive and outspoken. I didn't care for her or for the idea of her influencing my daughter.

"The next time she came to our house, she took me aside and said that she understood how I really felt about her. 'But for Sarah's sake, I hope you'll try to accept me for who I am,' she added. After she left the room, a voice within me demanded *Who are you who judges my child?* I was truly ashamed and prayed for forgiveness."

"Yet your repentance is incomplete," Sophia responds.

"I'm not sure what you mean. I felt terrible about what I'd done."

"Consider the widow who presided over a large household with gardens and livestock," invited Sophia. "When shearing time came, she said to her eldest son, 'Go out and work in the sheep barn today.' He smiled and said, 'I'm on my way, mother.' Then he went into town to dally with his friends. The widow then said to her second son, 'Go and work in the barn today.' Grimacing because he detested shearing, he replied, 'I can't. I have other things to do.' Later he regretted his words and went immediately to the sheep barn,"[1] Sophia narrates.

The Amma has no need to comment on the parable. Lucien sees that the second son is truly repentant not because he regrets his selfishness or says, "I'm sorry," but because he acts out his sorrow by doing his mother's will.

"From now on," Lucien says, "I will treat Sarah's friend as though she too were my daughter."

Sophia notes that repentance is good medicine for the heart, and recommends that Lucien not content himself with taking a small dose.

"Ask yourself *Why did I feel such antipathy for this girl? What is there of me in her that I need to forgive?* Perhaps your own assertiveness and frankness have wounded others. Or maybe these qualities—which are neither good nor bad in themselves—mar your image of yourself as a person of considerable charm with few detractors."

Judging by how offended he feels, Lucien knows that the Amma must be on target once again. With one hand held playfully over his heart, he says, "There is much more that needs forgiveness in here than I thought."

"Go to your Mother with it," Sophia advises.

"My Mother?"

"Have you forgotten who wept over unrepentant Israelites and yearned to gather them all under its wings like a mother hen?"

"I've never really related to that image of Jesus. Not virile enough for me, I suppose."

Standing and raising her arms in a powerful gesture, Sophia proclaims, "The sun of righteousness shall rise, with healing in its wings! And you shall tread down the wicked on the day when I act, says the Lord of hosts."[2]

Reproved, Lucien affirms that Jesus is both Mother Hen and Sun of Righteousness, Avenging Eagle and Poor Widow sweeping to find her lost coin.

"Take a lesson from the saints," Sophia instructs him. "Francis of Assisi required his friars to serve alternately as hermits and mothers who fed and cared for the hermits. Julian of Norwich insisted that Jesus is an all-loving Mother who harbors no anger against us. And Mechtild of Magdeburg saw God as our Mother 'who lifts her loved child from the ground to her knee.' "[3]

The Amma blesses Lucien and says, "Go to your Mother and be healed."

Bless the LORD, O my soul, and do not
forget all his benefits—
who forgives all your iniquity,
who heals all your diseases.
                                   Psalm 103:2-3

---

[1] See Matthew 21:28-32.

[2] See Malachi 4:2, 3.

[3] Matthew Fox, *Original Blessing* (Santa Fe: Bear & Co., 1983), p. 221.

8
THE COMPANY OF GOD'S FRIENDS

Sophia prescribes the medicine of friendship.

"TELL ME," SOPHIA INQUIRES, "how do you choose your friends?"

Lucien is surprised at himself for not having examined the question before. Considering it now, he realizes that he has employed friendship like a dragger's net, hauling in crustaceans and fish of various stripes. Looking closer at the catch, he sees that many are not friends but acquaintances serving his self-interests. Others are little more than social companions.

"Among your friends, Lucien, to whom can you entrust your heart?"

The Amma's second question is troubling. Other than his wife, Constance, there is no one before whom he would bare his true self. If any of his male friends were to overhear his dialogues with Sophia, Lucien would feel emasculated. To consult a priest is one thing. But a woman?

"The man who keeps himself covered in the presence of a spiritual friend is like the woman who refuses to disrobe in her doctor's office. Both deny themselves a salutary diagnosis," Sophia observes. "Wisdom assures us that a friend is the medicine of life. He or she points out hidden wounds and helps us treat them."

"I don't think I've ever had a friend who would risk calling me to account for my sins," Lucien responds, relishing the probable put-downs he would have administered to these would-be soul doctors.

"So you prefer to be a David with no Nathan to warn you as you rush toward the precipice with your eyes closed?"

Lucien concurs readily. "Perhaps I have chosen friends who were more apt to look up at me than straight across. I've counted on friends for affirmation—even flattery—rather than a frank assessment of how I'm doing spiritually. I'm not sure I'd know what to look for in a Nathan."

By way of response, Sophia describes her own soul friend, a woman of acute intellect and mild disposition. "As infirmities have restricted her physical range, she has grown correspondingly deep within. An hour spent with Beatrice is a respite under a sheltering tree. She affirms without falsity, corrects without wounding. We have been through many storms together and, as the wise person says, 'Friendship is made perfect by calamity.' "[1]

The Amma advises Lucien that in order to

find such a friend he must first become such a friend. As his guidebook, he is to consult *Spiritual Friendship*, the twelfth-century classic by Aelred of Rievaulx. There he will discover that the four basic virtues to be practiced by a true friend are loyalty, right intention, discretion and patience.[2]

If Lucien listens to his Cistercian guide, he will be formed as a faithful friend who, even when he is offended by another, does not withdraw his love. "Be concerned as much as you can for his welfare, safeguard his reputation, and never betray the secrets of his friendship," Aelred advises, "even though he should betray yours."[3]

The seeker begins to appreciate the gift and treasure of a friendship unadulterated by the poisonous additives of self-seeking, suspicion, backbiting, fear of disloyalty and harbored grudges.

Sophia reminds him that in some religious traditions, like the Eastern Orthodox, intercessory prayer for one's soul friend is considered the primary responsibility of both parties. "As Christ prayed for his friends on earth and as he 'always lives to make intercession' for us, so we must lift up those who share their hearts with us."[4]

Lucien can see that there might well be times when praying for a soul friend—truly seeing him, identifying with his need, speaking up for him to God—might be more profitable than time spent together hashing over a problem. He resolves to put into action Teresa of Avila's advice that if we want to grow in openness to God, we ought to seek the company of God's friends.[5]

By way of honing the seeker's decision, Sophia concludes with the story of Abba Sisoes who sees that one of his beloved disciples has been taken in by the devil's conniving. The Abba raises his arms toward heaven and says, "God, whether you will, or whether you will not, I will not let you alone until you have healed him." And on the spot the disciple is healed.[6]

> *...in every generation [Wisdom] passes*
>   *into holy souls*
> *and makes them friends of God, and*
>   *prophets.*
>
> Wisdom 7:27

[1] See Merton, *Way of Chuang Tzu*, p. 116.

[2] Aelred of Rievaulx, *Spiritual Friendship*, trans. Mary Eugenia Laker, S.S.N.D. (Kalamazoo, Mich.: Cistercian Pubs., 1977), p. 105.

[3] Ibid., p. 102.

[4] See Hebrews 7:25.

[5] Douglas V. Steere, "The Company of God's Friends," *Weavings*, Vol. III, No. 5 (Sept./Oct. 1988), p. 20.

[6] Sisoes 12, *The Sayings of the Desert Fathers: The Alphabetical Collection*, trans. Benedicta Ward, S.L.G. (London: A.R. Moubray and Co., Ltd., 1975), p. 180.

9
A COMMON LIFE

*Lucien focuses his
hunger for community.*

THE GENEROUS BOWLS OF BARLEY SOUP
and thick slices of grainy bread speak to
Lucien of how often and how eagerly Jesus sat at
table with his friends. Sharing Amma Sophia's
midday meal, he is aware of a long-denied
hunger. His heart, grown large with gratitude,
refuses to go on serving as a burial ground.

"Amma, give me a word that will console me
for the emptiness I feel at our parish liturgies."

"Did you come here to be healed or to receive
the last rites?" she inquires.

"Teach me then how to experience
community where I experience so much
alienation."

Although the disconnectedness of which
Lucien complains is not restricted to the Church,
it is there that it inflicts the greatest pain. Where
he hungers for fellowship, he confronts himself
alone in what seems a congregation of solitudes.

Sophia recalls an evening watching two
concerts on TV with friends. The first was a
twenty-fifth anniversary concert by a folk trio
who had remained faithful to their 1960s ideals
of a world without war and injustice.

"Their joyful rapport with the audience that
night was a sacrament, a sacred bond that

brought forth the goodness in each person and the presence of God in the gathering. The music, to which everyone knew the words, was prayer."

The second concert was a showcase for classical soloists of world renown. "I remember a pianist whose patrician demeanor and command of the keyboard awed the audience. They were mute before the perfection of the artist. And I remember how alone she was as she took her bows and departed."

Lucien considers Sophia's contrasting images as she continues, "Where celebrant and worshipers remain independent beings joined at the head for ritual, the fig tree blossoms not and Jesus goes hungry. But where believers recognize their mutual need and solidarity as pilgrims on the road to Jerusalem, all share in an abundant harvest."

"So how can I make the fig tree blossom?" Lucien wonders.

Like the folk trio, the disciples of Jesus had first to form community among themselves before they could unleash it in others. Sophia advises Lucien to actively seek, in his own parish or beyond, friends of God who will "leave their nets" long enough to build up a common life. They must make time to share food and stories, memories and resources, prayer and dreams.

"Do not lay down rules or formulate long-range plans. Allow the Holy Spirit to set your course. Wash one another's feet and sing one another's songs. Treat all as equals in the one Body."

Sophia's face glows as she contemplates the projected reality of "[W]here two or three are gathered in my name, I am there among them."[1]

The seeker is, however, bogged down in more pragmatic concerns. "Should we appoint a leader to delegate responsibilities and keep people motivated?" he asks, considering his own qualifications for the position.

"If a leader is required, you will know him or her by the latrine bucket in his or her hand."

Lucien laughs, convinced that Sophia is in jest.

"Have you never heard of the Indian wise man Vinoba Bhave? One day a visitor to the ashram was horrified to find Bhave emptying and cleaning the communal latrine buckets. The visitor insisted that such a sage should be out lecturing and passing on his great wisdom instead of performing such menial tasks. 'But'

Vinoba Bhave responded, 'since I help to fill the latrine buckets, why should I not help to empty them?' "[2]

This time Lucien's laughter is fitting for it is directed at his own urge to rise to the top. He admits to himself that one of his frustrations with parish liturgies is that he often thinks he might be a more effective celebrant than the vested one on the altar. With this thought, he quickly collects the lunch dishes and begins washing them.

As the disciple labors, Sophia gives him a prophecy. "In time your small community of love and others like it will cause the larger dough to rise. Be challenged by Clement of Alexandria who says, 'all our life is a festival: being persuaded that God is everywhere present on all sides, we praise [God] as we till the ground, we sing hymns as we sail the sea, we feel [God's] inspiration in all that we do."[3]

> ...[W]oe to one who is alone and falls
> and does not have another to help.
>
> Ecclesiastes 4:10

[1] Matthew 18:20.

[2] Donald Nicholl, *Holiness* (Mahwah, N.J.: Paulist Press, 1987), p. 126.

[3] Clement, "Stromateis," VII, vii, 35, in *The Library of Christian Classics*, Vol. II, *Alexandrian Christianity*, trans. Henry Chadwick and J.E.L. Oulton (Philadelphia: Westminster Press, 1954), p. 115.

<u>10</u>
WISDOM'S VESTURE

*Sophia bows deeply
to creation.*

B ROTHER SUN DISCREETLY AWAKENS the creatures of the forest as Sophia enters the still dark path. Lucien accompanies her, heavy footed and yawning, having risen before dawn to be here at this virgin hour. The Amma has insisted that he, a city dweller, must learn to savor nature if he would gain spiritual stature.

Sophia removes her sandals and sets them on a decaying stump. "Take off your shoes," she says, "so that you, like Moses at Horeb, may remember that you are walking on holy ground." The seeker complies despite his qualms about stinging insects, poisonous snakes and other wilderness threats of which he has limited knowledge.

As his toes become familiar with the cool, damp earth, Lucien feels reluctance slipping away. Sophia speaks in a hushed voice so as not to awaken a single bird or blade of grass before its time.

"All the great mystics counsel us to surrender to the glory of creation. If we fail to befriend the blessed works of God's hands, we are like amateur hikers who attempt to make our way through Denali National Park without benefit of trails or guides. Do you recognize any spiritual directors in the company around you?"

"What company, Amma? You and I are the only ones here."

Whispering in a peremptory tone, Sophia answers, "Blind seeker! Having taken off your shoes, will you now remove your blindfold?"

Anger at her tone awakens him, and for the first time, he becomes aware of the diaphanous world they have entered. Light glimmers through the gaps between spruce boughs and poplar branches. In silence, the sun rouses each being like an acolyte passing the paschal flame at Easter Vigil. In the far reaches of the cathedral, a thrush intones Prime and a bluejay confidently addresses an attentive Creator.

At Lucien's feet a patch of modest violets regards him as though aware of their kinship. He stoops down to smile at them and unexpectedly recalls a few lines from Baudelaire which he has formerly enjoyed for their sound without attending to their meaning: "We walk through forests of physical things/that are also spiritual things/that look on us with affectionate looks."[1]

Cradling the face of a single violet, Lucien allows himself to be a boyish lover. He regrets all the years of business and study during which he never sought out a mayflower or fed a goldfinch or planted an oak.

Pleased with Lucien's growing discernment, the Amma gives him a word from the mystic Mechtild of Magdeburg: "The truly wise person/ kneels at the feet of all creatures/and is not afraid to endure/the mockery of others."[2]

Mentor and seeker walk on together in silence as the wind heaves a gentle sigh on its way through the forest. A small brown rabbit aims his detecting ears at the visitors but senses no harm. Lucien breathes deeply and is glad to be in the temple.

Stretching her arms out toward the beauty before them, Sophia says, "Here is Wisdom's green and golden vesture. As Hildegarde perceived, it 'reveals the hidden God just as a person's clothes hint at his [her] body.' "[3]

Struck by the sensuality of this image, Lucien extends it by comparing Wisdom to the lover in the Song of Songs who peers through the lattices and says, "Arise and come."

Sophia agrees. "But how many miss the invitation because they are off to the office or the factory or the mall? Wisdom invites them to play with her in the greenery, dance with her under the stars, race with her on the beach. She offers to fill up their treasuries. Yet, they scurry away, saying 'Sorry. Too busy.' "

Lucien decides that he will not let a single week pass by without spending a few hours in Nature's company. Like Alan of Lille, he wants to see that "The whole created world is like a book, a picture, and a mirror for us."[4]

> *How desirable are all his works*
> *and how sparkling they are to see!*
> *...Who could ever tire of seeing his*
> *glory?*
>
> Sirach 42:22, 25

---

[1] Fox, *Original Blessing*, p. 38.

[2] Ibid., p. 69.

[3] Newman, *Sister of Wisdom*, p. 71.

[4] Ibid., p. 20.

11
ONE GRAIN OF TIME

*Lucien learns to live
in the* now.

"TELL ME, MY FRIEND, are you making progress in wisdom?" Sophia inquires.

Without hesitation, Lucien assures the Amma that he is no longer sick at heart, that he is adding beads to his string, and that he is eager to move on to greater enlightenment.

"On your way to the hermitage today, what did you see?"

Caught off beat, the seeker admits that in his eagerness to arrive, he paid little attention to the passing scene. He was focused on his destination.

"Had you taken more time, you might have arrived at your destination sooner," Sophia observes. She sets before Lucien a small hourglass.

"A renowned Zen master often asked his disciples, 'What, at this moment, is lacking?' How would you respond, Lucien?"

Connecting with the rhythm Sophia has introduced, Lucien allows the question to fall slowly into his deeper consciousness. Several minutes pass before he is sure of the answer.

"Nothing is lacking, Amma."

"You speak the truth, seeker. If you had known that secret when you arose this morning, you would have savored the beauty of your wife's face at the breakfast table, the sound of your children's voices, the silence inside your monk's cell as you drove your car, the traces of God in creation all along the way."

Lucien rebels at the impossibility of habitual awareness. He holds that it is only natural for our minds to scurry into the future or dawdle in the past when the now does not command attention.

Sophia responds, "Consider the pendulum which, as the clock master was about to repair it, spoke up saying, 'Please be kind and leave me as I am. I can't bear the thought of how many times I will have to tick hour after hour, day after day, year after year. It's just too much for me.' And the clock master said, 'Do not project yourself into the future. Just do one tick at a time and you will be able to enjoy each one.' "[1]

"This is all very good theoretically," Lucien responds, "but I don't believe it can be practiced except in a general way."

"Ah! Then what do you make of Jesus' admonition that we let tomorrow take care of itself? And what of the parables of watchfulness, of the wedding banquet and of the talents to be invested in the now? Does Jesus then require the impossible of us?"

Lucien is tempted to give a resounding "Yes!" Yet, he knows Matthew 19:26 ("For man it is impossible, but for God all things are possible") by heart, and knows, too, that Sophia has him pinned in good rabbinical fashion.

His mentor recalls the example of Brother Lawrence of the Resurrection who served as cook and cobbler for a twelfth-century Carmelite monastery. "He made it his life's work to keep continual company with God. By focusing on the present, he was able to stay within the still point at the core of his being. His awareness of the now was so complete that he could not recall what he had eaten for lunch once he had left the table."[2]

"My grandfather has that same problem," Lucien quips.

Sophia gives him a look that says "You are amusing, but stop evading the point." She recommends that he focus on the hourglass as a symbol of keeping time. Whenever he catches himself running greedily ahead or sliding into yesterday, he is to picture the hourglass.

"Concentrate on those few grains of sand held in abeyance at the neck just before they fall," she advises. "Image them motionless at the point where time stands still. Then stand at that same point and pray, 'God, you are here. Nothing is lacking.' "

Lucien sees how this practice—even when done sporadically—can be liberating. He might be freed of his constant frustration of "never enough time" and begin to experience the present as a congenial place for prayer. With pleasure, he suddenly recognizes the accuracy of Eckhart's, "God is at home; we are abroad."[3]

Laughing at the "coincidence" of Lucien's reference, Sophia makes him a gift of the hourglass and invites him to read the inscription she has placed on the bottom.

"God is always ready but we are not ready. God is near to us but we are far from him."[4]

For everything there is a season, and a
time for every matter under heaven:
a time to seek, and a time to lose;
a time to keep, and a time to throw
away;

Ecclesiastes 3:1, 6

[1] See de Mello, *Heart of the Enlightened*, p. 162.

[2] Brother Lawrence, *Daily Readings With Brother Lawrence* (Springfield, Ill.: Templegate Publishers, 1985), p. 39.

[3] Meister Eckhart, *Meister Eckhart: A Modern Translation*, trans. Raymond B. Blakney (New York: Harper & Row, 1941), p. 132.

[4] Ibid.

12
A DOOR TO
THE SACRED

*Sophia illuminates a
path of prayer.*

WHEN LUCIEN ARRIVES, the door of the hermitage chapel stands open, and he can see Sophia before a primitive altar. She has never before shown him the chapel, but he interprets the open door as an invitation to "come and see." Coughing inconspicuously, he enters and kneels opposite the Amma. A red lamp burns in the corner. Above the cedar tabernacle is a half-moon icon Lucien finds unusual.

Sophia nods in his direction but does not speak. Contenting himself with some deep breathing, Lucien studies the icon. In its center stands a Madonna with arms outstretched expansively and open palms raised in prayer. Her dark eyes confront the seeker directly; her lips are closed in a kindly expression.

Directly before the bosom of the Mother, his small arms mirroring her gesture, is the Son. While she prays for the world and presents the Savior to it, he extends two fingers of each hand in the attitude of a Teacher. Together they represent the fulfillment of Isaiah's prophecy: "Therefore the Lord himself will give you a sign. Look, the young woman is with child and shall bear a son, and shall name him Immanuel.' "[1]

In a hushed voice, Sophia explains that this is the Icon of the Sign, often found in Byzantine churches where, from the dome of the apse, it looks down on the altar and the community.

Lucien continues to gaze at the icon. Contrasting it with Madonna and Child paintings he favors, like Michelangelo's "Tondo Doni" and Corregio's "Virgin and Child," he finds it uninspiring. The Madonna, however, continues to regard him with undiscriminating interest.

He is relieved when Sophia leaves the chapel and invites him to join her at table. "Tell me, Lucien," she says, "the first time you saw your wife, did you absorb the full beauty of her character and the depth of her heart?"

"No, not at all," he responds. "I guess I'm still involved in that process."

"Nor does an icon give itself away on the first viewing. But if you keep on looking and living with it year after year, it will lead you into the heart of God."

She explains that an icon, unlike a religious masterpiece, is intended to portray the spiritual body rather than the physical body. It is not a likeness but a presence inviting a gaze. Church tradition sees the icon as a tangible sign of our relationship with God.

"Somehow I did not expect someone as advanced in prayer as you are, Amma, to be dependent on icons. I've always thought of religious art as a kind of crutch for those of us who are not true contemplatives."

With well-tried patience, Sophia responds, "Perhaps when I have surpassed such masters as Teresa of Avila and John Damascene—both of whom used and taught others to use icons—I shall have to consider your point. However, if this practice seems too elementary for you, take to heart the advice of Abbot Alonius who says, 'Humility is the land where God wants us to go and offer sacrifice.' "[2]

Having betrayed himself, Lucien makes amends without delay. "Teach me how to pray with an icon, Amma, and I will pray for humility," he adds with amusement.

"First, you must seek the right icon," Sophia responds. "Visit Eastern Orthodox churches. Meditate on books or catalogues of icons. Listen to your heart. Wisdom will point out to you that image by which you will be drawn into the Image of the Invisible God who is Christ our Lord."

The Amma's words trigger a memory from

his college years. In a text on comparative religions, he had come across a sixth-century icon that stunned him. He had never before envisioned Christ with such commanding beauty or undeniable authority.

Sophia immediately identifies Lucien's remembered image as Christ Pantocrator, Ruler of All, who blesses with one hand and holds the Book of the Gospels in the other. "If it is he who calls you," she says, "you will not have to worry about outgrowing your icon."

On his return trip to the city, Lucien feels the eyes of the Byzantine Madonna on him. "Mary," he prays, "show me the door you have prepared for me."

> *Happy is the person who meditates on*
> *   wisdom*
> *and reasons intelligently,*
> *who reflects in his heart on her ways*
> *   and ponders her secrets.*
>   Sirach 14:20-21

---

[1] Isaiah 7:14.

[2] Merton, *Wisdom of the Desert*, p. 53.

<u>13</u>
A Silent Lamp

*Sophia sheds more
light on prayer.*

LUCIEN PLACES THE SACRED IMAGE on the table before Amma Sophia. The Ruler of All is the bond between them. His face is human yet illuminated from within by the shekinah, the glory of God. "One thing I asked of the LORD," said the psalmist, "to behold the beauty of the LORD."[1] Since the day he acquired the icon, Lucien has made those words his own.

"Now that I have found this door to the sacred, how shall I integrate it into my prayer?" he asks. "I've made a place for it in my study, and I stand before it to offer morning or evening prayer from the Liturgy of the Hours. But then my attention is divided between the book and the face."

Sophia responds by offering him a round loaf of unsliced bread with his coffee. He defers, saying, "One piece will be enough for me."

"So it is with the Hours and the icon," the Amma observes. "Only one piece of the former is needful when praying with the latter. John Cassian recommends that whatever our prayer, we begin with the psalm verse, 'O God, come to my assistance. O Lord, make haste to help me.' "[2]

Sophia suggests that Lucien adopt the

Eastern custom of giving the icon a place of honor in his home where others will be affected by it. A small lamp or sanctuary candle should be placed before it as an invitation to prayer.

"As you become more intimate with the face of the Pantocrator, you will find that it encourages prayerful bows and kisses," she adds, smiling at Lucien's obvious discomfort.

Edging away from what he views as a feminine expression of devotion, Lucien inquires how he should proceed after the psalm verse.

"Why, become a silent lamp!"

Unsure of this enigmatic response, Lucien wonders whether Sophia is recommending a meditation on the face itself or on gospel passages that might come to mind.

"What does a lamp do?" she asks.

"It burns—and gives light."

"Take this word from Richard Rolle and put it into practice: 'God is all light and burning. The light clarifies our reason, while the burning kindles our desires, so that we desire nothing but him.' "[3]

With reverence, Lucien takes up the icon and enters the chapel. Placing the Pantocrator on the altar, Lucien sits with his back erect and his eyes closed, breathing deeply and attending to his breath.

In time he prays, "O God, come to my assistance. O Lord, make haste to help me."

Letting go, he slips into the silence and allows it to cover him. He gazes at the icon, trying not to entertain all the prayers and descriptive phrases that float across his mind like life rafts. "Be still," his heart commands. "A lamp says nothing."

The Pantocrator contemplates Lucien with love.

After an indiscernible period of time, the seeker becomes aware of a gentle voice behind him. Sophia is leading him out of the sea of silence. "He looks at me. I look at him. And we are happy," she says, in the words attributed to a peasant explaining to the Curé of Ars why he was spending hours before the tabernacle.

Lucien feels refreshed and calm at the core. He knows there will be times when silent prayer before the icon will seem like time wasted. But even when it does not feel like prayer, he will try to hang on to Christ's assurance: "All believing prayer is precious to me."[4]

Bowing over Sophia's hand, he kisses it lightly and says, "Thank you, Amma, for giving me new life."

She blesses him and presents him with a lovely strip of birch bark on which is written: "The human spirit is the lamp of the LORD, searching every inmost part."[5]

> *Your word is a lamp to my feet*
> *and a light to my path.*
>
> Psalm 119:105

---

[1] See Psalm 27:4.

[2] John Cassian, "Conference X on Prayer," *The Fire and the Cloud*, ed. David A. Fleming, S.M. (Mahwah, N.J.: Paulist Press, 1978), p. 35.

[3] Richard Rolle, "The Form of Perfect Living," 10, *Heart of the Saints*, ed. Francis W. Johnston (London: T. Shand Publishers, 1975), p. 316.

[4] Julian of Norwich, *Daily Readings*, p. 34.

[5] Proverbs 20:27.

14
WATERING GOD'S GARDEN

Lucien comes to understand compassion.

LUCIEN IS ASHAMED of what he must say. Yet, he knows that the doctor cannot treat an undeclared symptom. The Ruler of All has sent him out in search of less recognizable Christ faces. Sacrificing time he now thinks might have been better spent with his family, he has been serving dinner once a week in a Dorothy Day soup kitchen. The experience has left him angry and disillusioned.

"What did you expect to find when you went there?" Sophia inquires, with a hint of amusement in her voice.

"Christ," Lucien responds emphatically. "I expected to find him in those poor, homeless vagrants and winos and panhandlers."

"And what did you find?"

"Quite a number of self-centered, mean-spirited people who made me feel like they were doing me a favor allowing me to wait on them hand and foot. They have no more respect for the volunteers than they do for themselves. Not only were they not grateful, they actually laughed at me behind my back and joked about how long the newest 'pigeon' would last."

Noting the color in Lucien's face, Sophia inquires more gently, "How long will you last?"

The seeker admits that he has already cut back to serving once a month—at least until he can find a soup kitchen outside that particular inner-city slum. He is sure that the aggravation does him much less good than the same time invested in silent prayer.

Sophia responds with a story about a young monk who asks an elder, "Suppose there are two brothers and one of them prays and fasts all day in his cell, while the other visits the sick. Which one pleases God more?" And the elder responds, "If the one who prays and fasts six days a week were to hang himself up by the nose, he could not equal the one who attends to the sick."[1]

Lucien is convinced that the case is not that simple. He would be happy to visit the sick—he often does as a eucharistic minister for his parish. And even if he does not find a congenial soup kitchen, he will assuredly not neglect the poor.

"Would you be a Good Samaritan, Lucien?"

"No doubt every Christian would."

"Yes. And what does Luke tell us about the victim by the wayside? Was he worthy of the Samaritan's compassion? Did he show proper respect to his rescuer? Did he thank him and offer to repay all the money the Samaritan lavished on him? Or might he, in fact, have disdained the foreigner and thought him a fool for being so generous with no hope of a suitable recompense?"[2]

Lucien's silence says, "I hadn't looked at it that way before. Nor am I comforted to do so now."

The Amma leads the way out into the garden where she fills a large watering can and walks slowly among the outer rows of marigolds, bachelor's buttons and nasturtiums. Lucien occupies a weathered bench and watches without comment.

Indicating a wildflower trespassing among the marigolds, Sophia is careful to water even the cornflowers, though they intrude on the symmetry of her garden. "God's word," she says, "is like the rain that shows no partiality for the just or the unjust. Likewise, the Samaritan takes no notice of whether the needy one deserves his compassion or is grateful for it."

Sitting beside Lucien, the Amma continues, "When I encounter a poor person who repays my alms with skepticism or disdain, I remember the promise of Proverbs: '[O]ne who gives water will get water.'[3] And my resolution is strengthened by the psalmist who affirms that God is compassionate toward all God's works."[4]

Lucien's imagination recreates the hardened and defensive faces of the guests at the soup kitchen. He is shocked to see his own clean, well-rested face looking down on them from a great distance.

He wonders how different the faces would have looked had he allowed himself to identify with their destitution and empathized with their shame.

"There is a king in every man," Sophia tells him, quoting a Scandinavian proverb. "Speak to the king and the king will come forth."

Lucien smiles and takes his leave. He is almost beyond earshot when Sophia's voice reaches him once more. "When you return to the soup kitchen next week, my friend, you'll find the royalty you originally sought."

> *But the wisdom from above is first pure,*
> *then peaceable, gentle, willing to yield,*
> *full of mercy and good fruits, without a*
> *trace of partiality or hypocrisy.*
>
> James 3:17

[1] See Merton, *Wisdom of the Desert*, pp. 59, 60.

[2] See Luke 10:30-37.

[3] Proverbs 11:25.

[4] See Psalm 145:9.

15

ENCOUNTERING EVIL

*Lucien enlists in the cause
of justice and nonviolence.*

THERE ARE TIMES WHEN Lucien wishes he had remained content with his lukewarm spirituality. His prayer before the icon has borne prickly fruit. The more devoted he becomes to the Ruler of All, the less able he is to tolerate those who are ruled by a lust for power, possessions or violence. Watching the evening news is like hearing a shrill alarm and having no way to put out the fire.

Sophia, reading contention in his face, prepares a balm of wisdom sources. She begins with Francis of Assisi who has reappeared throughout Lucien's life as a mentor. Referring to the story of Francis' befriending the ravenous Wolf of Gubbio to reconcile the animal with the villagers, she asks, "What was it the people of Gubbio feared?"[1]

"Appearing as the entrée on the wolf's dinner menu," Lucien responds, laughing at the simplicity of the question.

"Was it the beast in the forest they feared or the beast in themselves? Perhaps the villagers, like you and me, feared their own animal nature out of which violence and rapacity arise. Unable to live with so intimate an anxiety, they projected it onto the wolf who could then be justifiably destroyed."

"So you see the wolf as a scapegoat?" Lucien asks.

"More than that. He's as much a spirit guide as Francis in this story. He acknowledges his guilt, places his trust in this emissary from the enemy camp and takes a vow of nonviolence to which he remains faithful until death."

Lucien's amusement at this interpretation makes him all the more amenable to what will follow. Sensing that he is ready to become a warrior, Sophia gives him a word that may prompt enlistment.

"Centuries ago during a civil war in an Asian country, there was a general who led his troops through one province after another, killing and destroying at will. Forewarned of his approach, the people of one small village ran off to the mountains to hide. The general was incensed when he found the village empty, so he ordered his soldiers to search every nook and cranny. They reported that there was but one person left in the entire area—and he was a Zen priest.

"The general strode up to confront the priest, unsheathed his sword, and said, 'Don't you know who I am? I am the one who can run you through without batting an eye.' The priest looked back at him and replied, 'And I, sir, am one who can be run through without batting an eye.' With that, the general bowed and left."[2]

The seeker smiles in admiration. "That's the kind of priest I'd love to meet," he remarks.

"Not only have you already met such a priest," Sophia says, "you can become one if you will."

Her meaning is not lost on Lucien. Isaiah's image of the Suffering Servant comes immediately to mind. Jesus is the Priest who does no violence, yet bears the guilt of the violent for their salvation. Gandhi, King, Romero, the Four Women Martyrs of El Salvador and thousands of others whose names Lucien does not know, all are warrior-priests who "can be run through."

"When you watch the generals and the politicians and the corporate chiefs on the evening news," Sophia asks, "what do you do with all the injustice you perceive?"

"I revile it and reject it. I hold it at arm's length and tell myself, 'See what new depths of inhumanity these bastards have sunk to now,'" Lucien responds, holding nothing back.

"And in this act of judgment and rejection, Lucien, you guarantee that the very injustice you wish to destroy will instead grow stronger."

Sophia recalls a powerful word from the spiritual master, Thomas Merton: "We are sinners and we have to be very glad to take upon ourselves all the evil in the world as if we were responsible for it ourselves, and to love everyone else in their sins. In this way only is evil overcome and destroyed."[3]

Lucien's stomach rebels at this hard-shelled truth. He has never been good at turning the other cheek or praying for the persecutors of this world. These strategies require heroic humility, self-discipline, inner surety and love that stands firm before the firing squad and the nails.

Sophia takes Lucien's hands in hers, and together they pray in silence. Her final word summons him to the battle.

"Blessed is the person, Lucien, who sees the sin and the salvation of others as though they were his own."

Out of his anguish he shall see light;
he shall find satisfaction through his knowledge.
The righteous one, my servant, shall

*make many righteous
and he shall bear their iniquities.*

Isaiah 53:11

---

[1] *St. Francis of Assisi: The Omnibus of Sources* (Chicago: Franciscan Herald Press, 1983), p. 1348.

[2] See Joseph Goldstein and Jack Kornfield, *Seeking the Heart of Wisdom: The Path of Insight Meditation* (Boston: Shambhala Publications, Inc., 1987), p. 76.

[3] Thomas Merton, *The Hidden Ground of Love: The Letters of Thomas Merton*, ed. William H. Shannon (New York: Farrar, Straus, Giroux, 1985), p. 388.

16
THE CALL TO
A SIMPLER LIFE

Sophia invites Lucien
to empty his boat.

AMMA SOPHIA IS WRAPPING A GIFT as Lucien arrives. When he inquires about it, she explains that it is for a young deacon friend who is about to be ordained a priest.

"And what is this gift, if I may ask?"

"My Icon of the Sign," she replies in a voice that reveals how pleased she is with her decision. Lucien, on the other hand, is perturbed that she would give away something of such spiritual value to herself.

"What then would you make of the Desert Father who sold his only copy of the book of the Gospels and used the money to feed the hungry because the book told him to sell all that he had and give to the poor?"[1]

The seeker frowns at such impractical wisdom and is relieved that it has not occurred to Sophia to sell the hermitage to help the homeless. "What do you own that you could not give away?" she inquires.

Lucien admits that the list would be substantial and would include everything from his wedding ring to his old golf clubs. "But you wouldn't catch me giving my icon away either," he remarks. "Not after all we've been through together."

Sophia smiles at Lucien's levity but is not put off the track. She describes how Sophocles lived so simply that he did not have a single pair of sandals. However, he was not entirely free of the spell of the marketplace. "He was repeatedly attracted there to gaze at all the products on display. When a friend noticed that Sophocles always came home empty-handed, he inquired about it. And the philosopher said, 'I love to go there and discover how many things I am perfectly happy without."[2]

"I'll try to remember that the next time my family and I are spending Saturday morning at the mall," Lucien responds with the same imperviousness to his mentor's intent.

"Consider this, Lucien. Does your comparative wealth cause envy among your relatives, coworkers or neighbors? Does it encourage your family to acquire and rely on more possessions than they need? Does it require you to spend more time and energy than you would like in securing, protecting and preserving it?"

There is a storm brewing in Lucien's heart, and he is angry at Sophia for arousing it. But recalling his new commitment to nonviolence, he simply insists that what he owns does not necessarily own him.

Despite the seeker's reluctance, Sophia requires him to consider also how his material comfort contributes to the poverty of the disenfranchised and the profits of unjust corporations.

"Amma, I can't concern myself with all of that. I'm only an individual—and not a wealthy one at that."

"Have you ever wondered about the rich young man who turned and walked away when Jesus challenged him to let go of his riches? Perhaps one of the reasons Jesus was so saddened by the young man's departure was that the man failed to see the connection between his own wealth and the poverty of those he was being challenged to enrich."[3]

Lucien says nothing. However, his resistance is less determined, and Sophia is not yet ready to let him go. She gives him a word from the eighteenth-century Quaker divine John Woolman who, in commenting on English economic abuse of Native Americans, wrote: "We cannot go into Superfluities, or grasp after Wealth in a Way contrary to [God's] Wisdom, without having Connection with some Degree of Oppression."[4]

The seeker decides that a walk in the woods will allow him to mull over the Amma's call to a simpler life more in harmony with the world's realities and the gospel's demands.

When he returns later, there is a note for him on the table.

"Chuang Tzu advises, 'If you can empty your own boat/Crossing the river of the world,/No one will oppose you,/No one will seek to harm you.' Notice that he did not say we should toss everything overboard at one time. Pax, Sophia."[5]

> *For freedom Christ has set us free.*
> *Stand firm, therefore, and do not submit*
> *again to a yoke of slavery.*
>
> Galatians 5:1

---

[1] See Merton, *Wisdom of the Desert*, p. 37.

[2] See de Mello, *Heart of the Enlightened*, p. 27.

[3] See Matthew 19:21-24.

[4] John Woolman, "Wealth and Oppression," *Daily Readings from Quaker Spirituality* (Springfield, Ill.: Templegate Publishers, 1987), p. 31.

[5] Merton, *Way of Chuang Tzu*, p. 114.

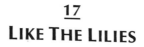

17
LIKE THE LILIES

*Sophia recommends
impartial gratitude.*

"PRAY FOR ME, AMMA. I can't even begin to empty my boat," Lucien begins, appealing for maternal sympathy.

"No, I will not. You are a man in a leaky canoe who shouts for help instead of bailing himself out. Until you pick up a bucket and start bailing, neither I nor God will help you."

Lucien feels compelled to justify himself by recounting the impoverished circumstances in which he grew up, the shame of having the family car repossessed, the lies to his friends. Now that he has made his own family secure through his own good stewardship, he has a responsibility to provide for them as best he can.

Sophia's response is a question: "Suppose you had an income of $125,000, and it was suddenly cut to $50,000. Would it be wiser to bemoan your loss or be comforted by the income you still had?"

"I should, of course, be grateful for the $50,000. Yet if my neighbor were still living on $125,000, I couldn't help complaining about my loss," Lucien says.

"Suppose the neighbor on your left inherited a mansion while the one on your right is about to suffer a foreclosure. To which will you compare your own circumstances?"

Lucien concedes the point.

"Let your family be guided by Solomon who insists that when the days of adversity come, we should not forget the days of prosperity and the pleasure we took in them."[1]

The seeker agrees, for he knows that he and his wife are more apt to exaggerate their losses than to resurrect gratitude for past blessings.

"When all is going well, Lucien, be at peace with what is given. But when what is given is suffering or diminishment, be equally at peace. Gratitude looks not just at the gift but the Giver. It says not only 'Thank you' but 'Let it be done.' "

"This is a tall order—to be as happy and grateful for nothing as for something," Lucien responds in a skeptical voice.

The Amma corrects him with a story about a Buddhist holy person whose only possession was a golden begging bowl presented to him by the King. Once, when he was about to settle down for the night in a ruined monastery, the holy one spotted a thief waiting to take advantage of him. "Take this bowl now," he said to the thief, "so you won't disturb my sleep later."

Sophia adds that the next morning the thief reappeared to return the bowl, saying, "Teach me how to acquire the riches that make this kind of lighthearted detachment possible."[2]

Lucien appreciates the story and is envious of the Buddhist's ability to let go gracefully. However, he finds it impossible to picture himself either giving the bowl away or being grateful for the opportunity.

The Amma tries a different approach. "Suppose, Lucien, that you give your son a wonderful set of blocks for Christmas. However, he does not praise the gift or the giver. Yet, when another child wants to share the blocks, your son refuses to let go of even a few."

Seeing himself in the ungrateful son, Lucien recalls a mystic's insight: "If the only prayer you say in your entire life is 'thank you,' that would suffice."[3] He resolves to live by this word.

"You said earlier that it is your responsibility to preserve your family's material comfort," Sophia observes. "But what of your responsibility to the Rabbi who urges you to take a lesson from the lilies of the field? No more anxiety about comparative riches! Break forth in blossoms of praise and thanks!"

The seeker squirms at this poetical piece of advice.

"Are you any less destined for praise than the psalmist or the contemporary poet?" Sophia inquires. "Do not silence in your heart that same fiery Spirit that moved Hildegard to sing, 'O power of Wisdom!/You encompassed the cosmos,/encircling and embracing all.../Praise to you, Wisdom, fitting praise!' "[4]

Laughing at his own inhibitions, Lucien clears his throat and sings in a decidedly masculine baritone: "Now thank we all our God, with hearts and hands and voices." Sophia joins in, doubling the seeker's joy.

> *Send out fragrance like incense,*
> *and put forth blossoms like a lily.*
> *Scatter the fragrance, and sing a hymn of*
> *praise;*
> *bless the Lord for all his works.*
> Sirach 39:14

---

[1] See Ecclesiastes 7:14.

[2] See de Mello, *Heart of the Enlightened*, pp. 30-31.

[3] Fox, *Original Blessing*, p. 115.

[4] Newman, *Sister of Wisdom*, p. 64.

18

THE JOURNEY BEGINS

*Lucien proclaims his
'Yes' to life.*

SOPHIA INITIATES THEIR final healing session with a story told by naturalist and essayist Loren Eiseley. Lucien is attentive, knowing that he will soon miss the sound of her voice.

"Once when Eiseley was staying in a seaside town where, suffering from insomnia, he would rise early and walk the beach at sunrise, he was saddened by the daily crowd gathering starfish to sell. Their single-mindedness seemed to him a sign of the many ways the world says 'no' to life."

Lucien instinctively identifies with the enterprising townsfolk who are out to make an extra dollar—but he says nothing.

"One morning Eiseley got down to the beach before sunrise. There he saw a solitary man picking up starfish and throwing them back into the safety of the sea. Heartened by the sight, Eiseley returned at that same time seven mornings in a row. Each time the 'star thrower' was there, pursuing his mission of mercy. And the naturalist found himself wondering if there was a star thrower at work in the universe, a God who contradicts death, and whose nature is pure mercy."[1]

Upon hearing this conclusion, Lucien

resolves to nourish the star thrower in himself and his children.

Sophia reminds him that there are many ways to "choose life" and the choice must be eternally renewed. When Lucien finds himself slipping into the ways of death that sicken the heart, he must stop and be present to God who is always at home.

The Amma gives Lucien a word from essayist Annie Dillard: "Experiencing the present purely is being emptied and hollow; you catch grace as a man fills his cup under a waterfall."[2]

Lucien imagines himself with a cup flowing over, and he resolves to be present to life as it is given.

Sophia now invites him to consider a third source of wisdom in inspired literature.

"Consider, Lucien, what those who are dying most regret as they prepare to say 'It is finished.' Tolstoy provides the answer in his story of a middle-aged magistrate who adopts the values of the upper classes, discreetly enjoys having power over others and invests himself in his career rather than his family relationships. Living beyond his means, Iván Ilych considers himself to be happy.

"However, a fatal illness forces him to realize that he has poisoned his own life and now has no one to pity or console him. He is repelled by death and the terrible 'mesh of falsity' he is trapped in. Finally, through the ministrations of a humble servant, Iván Ilych is able to repent and say 'Yes'—not to death, for he discovers that death 'is no more'[3]—but to the life that should have been his."

Lucien understands and resolves to judge the rightness of his own life by Wisdom's counsels rather than the world's standards.

"Finally, Lucien, whatever ailments assail you, keep before your eyes the witness of Jesus who in his flesh was never anything but 'yes' to God...in the starfish and the lily...in the prostitute and the tax collector...in the sick and the sick at heart. He was 'yes' to God in the death that gives life."

Sophia anoints Lucien's forehead and hands, saying, "Seeker of light, may you dwell forever in the house of Wisdom."

Blessing the Amma in return, Lucien prays, "May the Spirit empower you to heal many hearts as you have healed mine."

After embracing the Amma, Lucien turns to set his feet on the path she has illuminated.

*...Jesus Christ...was not "Yes and No";
but in him it is always "Yes."*

2 Corinthians 1:19

---

1 Parker J. Palmer, "The Stations of the Cross," *Weavings*, Vol. VI, No. 2 (March/April 1991), p. 17.

2 Annie Dillard, *Pilgrim at Tinker Creek* (New York: Harper's Magazine Press, 1974), pp. 80-81.

3 Leo Tolstoy, "The Death of Iván Ilych," *The Death of Iván Ilych and Other Stories* (New York: New American Library, 1960), p. 156.

Suggested Resources

Daily Readings with Julian of Norwich, Volumes 1 and 2. Springfield, Ill.: Templegate Publishers, 1980.

de Mello, Anthony, S.J. *The Heart of the Enlightened: A Book of Story Meditations*. New York: Doubleday, 1989.

Goldstein, Joseph and Jack Kornfield. *Seeking the Heart of Wisdom: The Path of Insight Meditation*. Boston: Shambhala Publications, Inc., 1987.

Meister Eckhart: A Modern Translation, trans. Raymond B. Blakney. New York: Harper & Row, 1941.

Merton, Thomas. *The Wisdom of the Desert: Some Sayings of the Desert Fathers*. New York: New Directions Pub. Corp., 1960.

Newman, Barbara. *Sister of Wisdom: St. Hildegard's Theology of the Feminine*. Berkeley: University of California Press, 1987.